My Donkey

GREGORY GRANT

Ordering Information:

Prime Seven Media
518 Landmann St.
Tomah City, WI 54660

Printed in the United States of America

My Donkey

His name is Sam the donkey he carries me up and down hills he is my only way to get to places, my name is Greg the helpful one. My donkey will carry me and my tent for me incase we have to sleep out,

Which we did one night to help this farmer by the name of Thomas his herd of sheep went missing. He was driving them up they usally route up the hill that they call the Disappearing Hill, they called it so because everything disappears on it.

When he heard his phone ringing, he answered it and when he came back they were gone. So I said, "I will look at first light" so I set up me tent in the paddock and tied up Sam on the fance posted and went to sleep.

The next day, I got up and had breakfast which was just Beacon and eggs. Me and Sam set out to look for Thomas sheep. So we looked here we looked their and no sheep to be found, but strange I saw a key on the ground but no door in sight, so I went to Thomas farmhouse and asked him what is this key for but he had no idea, but he did say that there is a story of a hidden door within the hill were this robber is by the name of Gregor the Terrible lives and he has claimed the hill to be has and every thing that walks on it human or animal shall be his.

So I went back to the hill to try to find this door but with no success so I thought I leave it until tomorrow, so I went back to the tent to get ready for dinner which Thomas invited me over to his place for tea. So I got ready and went over, when I got there, I noticed he had a picture of a woman, on his wall in the T.V room he said that was of his wife so I ask what happened, he said "that one day she was driving the sheep with me and I turned my back for a minute and she was gone, it has now been over five years to the day and nobody knows where she is."

We sit down to a nice roast lamb, so we also had a few drinks and talked I told him about my wife, how she died in an accident a herd of wild horses running her over there was a motor bike frighten, the horses and she was in their path her name was Annie.

So, then I went back to find that some one has been in my tent, probably looking for that key. It was a mess. My sleeping bag was thrown out, the tent was almost fallen over so I set it up again then went down to look at Sam, but he was fine chewing grass.

The next day after breakfast, I got Sam and begin to look for this door, so we brave the hill it took us a while, but we finely found this door. It was a huge door and I through this door must belong to 'Gregor the Terrible'. So I put the key in the slot and it fitted so I turn it and it opened, me and the donkey rode through the doorway and it was the mirror image of what was outside, there was a shed, farm house and green hills, before I went further I turn around and went back to me tent to get a few things that I would need.

When I got everything, I had a bit to eat, then headed back to the door with Sam, I opened the door and rode in. I rode toward the shed hoping that the lost sheep were in their, but there were no sheep but I did hear another noise, it was coming from somewhere in the shed, so I looked everywhere and found nothing there were a bundle of hay on the floor so I moved that and I found there was a trap door, I opened the trap door shone a light through dark and keep on hearing the noise, there was a women tied up in the comer. So I got some rope from the bundles of hay and tied it around one of the pile and lower myself down, I got down their and started to untie this woman, and the rope that I climbed down on fell to the ground and then the trap down shut, I looked for a another way out but there was none, but there was a spike on a handle on the ground, so I pick it up with the rope that fall to the ground, I climbed on some hey and reached the top but the trap down was shut tight, so I got the spike and jammed it in the crack to try and leaver it up open but I couldn't.

Then I smelled smoke coming though the crack of the walls so now I have to act quickly So I call to Sam the donkey and yes he heard me, and told Sam to kick the trap door in which he did, when the trapped door falls to ground I got the woman and climbed out of there, we than got on the donkey on rode out of them.

NTHOU

After we got clear of the hey shed we got talking and it turns out that the woman was the farmers Thomas wife Clara, I told Clare that I will ride you back to the door and go back to Thomas She said "thank you" and gave me a kiss.

Now with her gone, Sam and I continue to look for the sheep, I got back on Sam and we rode around the farm, no sign of the sheep I saw a well so I rode up for a closer look I got off Sam and looked in, it was bone dry just as I was about to turn around to get back on

Sam, someone pushed me in the back, and I fell in. It was about a 20 meter drop and I had no way of getting out, lucky I didn't break anything, the wall of the well had stepping stones build into it, so I started to climb up them when I got out of the well I got on Sam and rode away from them.

The next place I looked for the sheep was a dam, they weren't in their but I saw some one from the corner of my eye, whoever it was they were going toward a field full of wheat, so I rode in looking for him, it was a tall man it could have been Gregor the terrible.

He was hard to follow being so tall he must have been nearly six foot; he was also a very fast runner for a giant lucky I was on a very fast donkey so I kicked Sam to go faster, but we still couldn't catch him so we let him go I said, "that we will catch him latter.

So I continue my ride looking for the sheep, my look took me to an old unused farm house, I had a look inside it look like who ever used to live here left in a hurry there was mess everywhere, but looking further I found a made up bed and a chair, outside was a boy smoking as I approached him he notices and tried to run put he didn't get far he had a ball and chain on, So I asked who he was and he answered that his name was William, he was kidnapped by Gregor the terrible and brought here, "I came in, when I saw him, with the sheep and my mother Clare."

So, you Thomas son "yes" he said, I got a knife which was in one of the draws and break the lock on the ball and chain and took him to Sam.

We then rode two the hey Shed that was nearly burn down and hide William where the trapped door was and put hay bundles around it, I said, "that I will be back in a few minutes." He asked were I going? I said, "I think we were followed."

I was right we were followed by a man wearing a black coat ridding a purple horse, I said" Now I seen everything" when he saw me, he turns and rode away.

I went back to William; William asked, "Who was that?" I said, "Just a mans in a black coat riding a purple horse." William told me that his name is "The Purple Shepard and he is the one that help Gregor the Terrible able kidnapped the sheep." So I figured if I find The Purple Shepard I find Grego the Terrible and the sheep, but first I have to get William home without being followed again which will be heard since he is watching our every move, so I waited until dark and then I sneak outside and had a look and the coast was clear, so I got William and got on Sam and rode to the door, opened it and William said "Thank you" then walked through the door.

When he was gone I rode back the to shed still no Purple Shepard, I then I made myself at home just then I hear a noise it was coming from outside it was Sam the donkey putting up a fight the Purple Shepard was trying to take him. That donkey of mine is a biter I whistle to him to come over. So, I got on and followed the Purple Shepard.

Hopefully the Purple Shepard who was on horse would lead me to the Giant Gregor the Terrible and the sheep.

He leads me through the wheat field past, the well and back to the unused farm house, he went in I followed him and he made a phone call, I say it was to Gregor the terrible he said, "That William was gone, the guy on the donkey took him I think he is in the shed."

I came out of the crack, I was hiding in, got on Sam and followed The Purple Sheppard he leads me to a castle, Sam and I went into the courtyard, but no one was around, then the drawbridge went up and I had a feeling we were court, suddenly a loud voice came from now where laughing "HA, HA, HA, I had been waiting for you

Greg the Help for one, then a few of the Giant's security guard's grab me pulling me of Sam, I hit the ground and they dragged me too the Duncan, were they handicapped me to these chains. Throw the keys on the ground after chaining me up and said as they walk away, "Now try to get these Ha

Ha." Then slam the door shut, the chains were on a puller system so I pulled one arm and found out that if I pulled hard enough I should be able to reach the keys and then I could release the pulley.

So that is what I did it took me a few goes but I got there and go the keys and undone the handcuffed, unlocking the door. I run down the corridor door but was confronted by some more guards, so I turn back to run the other way to get rid of them I went back in the Dungan and the guards followed me in so I quickly ran back out locking the door behind me.

On my way back to look for the Giant I heard a noise it sounded like sheep coming from the caller I through "Great, I found the sheep" So I went in to get the sheep out, but as quickly as I went the the door slammed shut, there was an air vent up above us the caller walls were brick but in a stepping stone effect so I clamed up the wall and kick the covered of the air vent and climbed inside and curl to the other air vent covered which was on the outside of the caller, so kicking that air vent cover to the ground I got down and unlock the door sally people left the key in and I got the sheep out.

Now With the Sheep, I went to get Sam who was tied up in the courtyard under guard when I got their they were try to keep Sam quite but giving him some hey but he was mad, I throw a stone to get Sam attention which it did I gave him the signal to kick the guard in the back so I could ran over and untie Sam, when he kick the guard he fell to the ground, I ran in untie Sam and tie up the guard then got on Sam and got to the Sheep and started to go out releasing that the drawbridge which was closed, So I had some TNT just_in case on Sam and I put the TNT under to draw bridge hoping it will blow over the ditch which it did, so back on Sam we rod out with the sheep half way to the wall, the guards came after me. So I kicked Sam into high guard with the sheep we just went and leaf he others of dead we past the wall and field of wheat which the disused farm house with the shed which was nearly burnt down with us inside finally got to the door I opened it and we three went through it, I close it behind me and made shore it could never be opened again, then Sam and I took the sheep to Thomas the farmer, Thomas was gratefully and offer money but we dint expected it, then offer us Tea, which we did excepted so I went in and they got Sam some Water and a few greens.

The next day I packed up the tent loaded it onto Sam and rode away to the next job.

The End